Dedicated to

Anika Margaret Carlson

ZONDERKIDZ

Goodnight, Angels
Copyright© 2011 by Melody Carlson
Illustrations© 2011 by Sophie Allsopp

Requests for information should be addressed to:

Zonderkidz, Grand Rapids, Michigan 49530

Library of Congress Cataloging-in-Publication Data
Carlson, Melody.
    Goodnight, angels / by Melody Carlson ; [illustrations by Sophie Allsopp].
       p.   cm.
       Summary: Rhyming text follows a child who is saying goodnight to everyone and everything,
from friends to a toothbrush to Father God and the angels.
       ISBN 978-0-310-71687-7 (hardcover)
       [1. Stories in rhyme. 2. Bedtime—Fiction 3. Christian life—Fiction.] I. Allsopp, Sophie, ill.
II. Title. III. Title: Good night, angels.
    PZ8.3.C214Goo 2012
    [E]—dc22   2008048896

Zonderkidz is a trademark of Zondervan.

Editor: Barbara Herndon
Art direction: Sarah Molegraaf
Design: Cindy Davis

Printed in China

11 12 13 14 15 16 /LPC/ 6 5 4 3 2 1

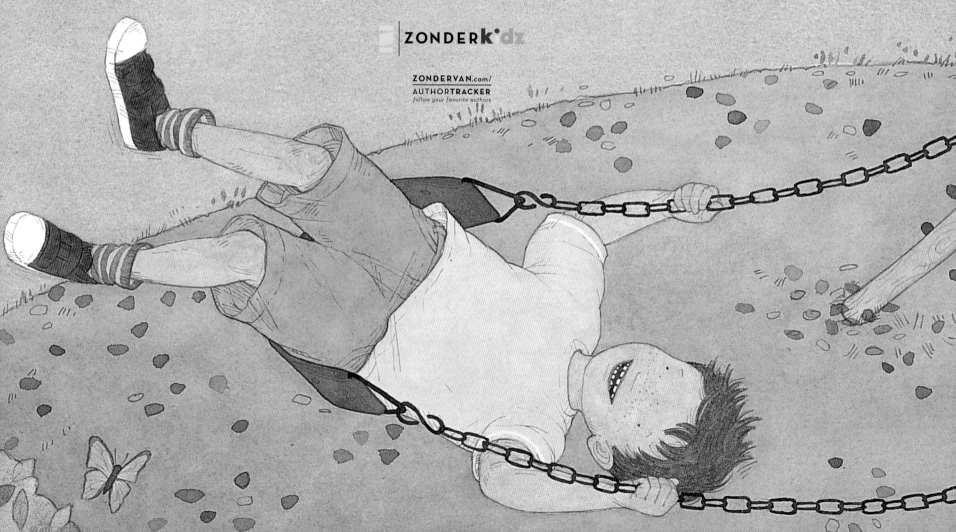

Goodnight, Angels

Story by Melody Carlson

Pictures by Sophie Allsopp

ZONDERkidz

ZONDERVAN.com/
AUTHORTRACKER
follow your favorite authors

Goodnight to the bird and the butterfly.
Goodnight to my friends. I have to say goodbye.

Goodnight to my wagon. Didn't we have fun?

Goodnight to the big clouds and sinking sun.

8

Goodnight to my kitty, sleeping on the rug.
Goodnight to my doggy. Here's a nice big hug.

11

Goodnight to the last bit of my bedtime snack.

Goodnight to the kitchen. Tomorrow I'll be back.

Goodnight, rubber duckie. Thank you for the scrub.
Goodnight to the bubbles, sliding down the tub.

14

Goodnight to my toothbrush. Goodnight to the sink.
Goodnight to my little cup that holds my bedtime drink.

Goodnight, bunny slippers, snuggling 'neath my bed.
Goodnight, Mister Teddy. You're a sleepyhead.

18

19

Goodnight to my daddy. And if it's not too late ...

How about a story? One with bears is great!

21

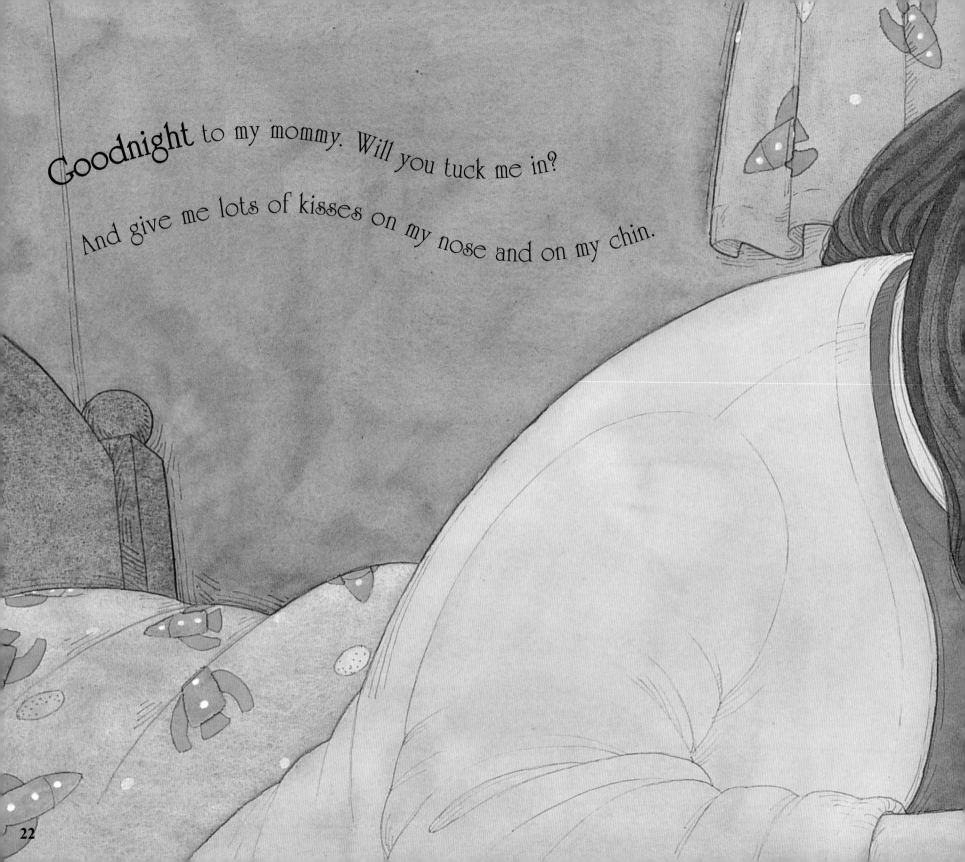

Goodnight to my mommy. Will you tuck me in?

And give me lots of kisses on my nose and on my chin.

23

Goodnight to my nightlight, glowing in my room.

Goodnight to the starry sky. Goodnight, yellow moon.

Goodnight, Father God. Here's my bedtime prayer.

Thank you for your blessings ... for your love and care.

27

Goodnight to the quiet night. My eyes are getting sleepy.

Goodnight to the angels ... watching over me.

28